STEP 2

READING WITH HELP

STEP INTO READING

This Makes Me Jealous

DEALING WITH FEELINGS

by Courtney Carbone

illustrated by Hilli Kushnir

Random House 🏠 New York

A new girl named Amy
came to school today.

She walked in
during my show-and-tell!

Everyone ignored me
and stared at her.

I felt as prickly
as my cactus plant.

My teacher asked me
to share my desk.

I did not like having
to share my things.

The other kids crowded
around Amy at recess.

I did not see
what the big deal was.

Next we played soccer
in gym class.

It was my turn
to be the goalie.

But Amy made me
look bad.

She scored a goal
on her very first kick.

"Hooray!"
everyone cheered.

I felt like the ball
hit me in the stomach.

I stomped off the field.

My teacher stopped me.
She asked what was wrong.

I thought about my day.
I thought about Amy.

How was I feeling?
I was feeling JEALOUS.

My teacher listened.
She nodded.

She then asked me
how *Amy* must feel.

I had not thought
about how Amy felt.
It must be hard
to be the new kid.

My teacher asked me
what I could do to help.

I said I would try
to be a friend to Amy.

I found Amy
near our desk.

I shared my paints.
We started to talk.

Soon we were laughing
and having fun.

I barely noticed
when the bell rang!

I am glad I gave
Amy a chance.

I think we will be
good friends after all.

For anyone who needs a friend, that they may be a friend

—C.B.C.

To Liam and Aya, my team of bandits and partners in crime

—H.K.

Text copyright © 2019 by Courtney Carbone
Cover art and interior illustrations copyright © 2019 by Hilli Kushnir

Visit us on the Web!
StepIntoReading.com
rhcbooks.com

Educators and librarians, for a variety of teaching tools, visit us at
RHTeachersLibrarians.com

Library of Congress Cataloging-in-Publication Data is available upon request.
ISBN 978-0-593-48183-7 (trade) — ISBN 978-0-593-48184-4 (lib. bdg.) —
ISBN 978-0-593-48185-1 (ebook)

Printed in the United States of America
10 9 8 7 6 5 4 3 2 1

This book has been officially leveled by using the F&P Text Level Gradient™ Leveling System.